JOHN ADAMS

by Ellis M. Reed

Cody Koala
An Imprint of Pop!
popbooksonline.com

abdopublishing.com
Published by Pop!, a division of ABDO, PO Box 398166, Minneapolis, Minnesota 55439. Copyright © 2019 by POP, LLC. International copyrights reserved in all countries. No part of this book may be reproduced in any form without written permission from the publisher. Pop!™ is a trademark and logo of POP, LLC.

Printed in the United States of America, North Mankato, Minnesota

032018
092018

THIS BOOK CONTAINS
RECYCLED MATERIALS

Cover Photo: Shutterstock Images
Interior Photos: Shutterstock Images, 1, 5, 6, 9, 14, 17 (bottom right), 19, 20 (top left); iStockphoto, 10; North Wind Picture Archives, 13, 17 (top), 17 (bottom left), 20 (bottom), 21 (top right)

Editor: Charly Haley
Series Designer: Laura Mitchell

Library of Congress Control Number: 2017963378
Publisher's Cataloging-in-Publication Data
Names: Reed, Ellis M., author.
Title: John Adams / by Ellis M. Reed.
Description: Minneapolis, Minnesota : Pop!, 2019. | Series: Founding fathers | Includes online resources and index.
Identifiers: ISBN 9781532160172 (lib.bdg.) | ISBN 9781532161292 (ebook) |
Subjects: LCSH: Adams, John, 1735-1826--Juvenile literature. | Founding Fathers of the United States--Juvenile literature. | Statesmen--United States--Biography--Juvenile literature. | United States--Politics and government--1783-1789--Juvenile literature.
Classification: DDC 973.4 [B]--dc23

Hello! My name is

Cody Koala

Pop open this book and you'll find QR codes like this one, loaded with information, so you can learn even more!

Scan this code* and others like it while you read,

or visit the website below to make this book pop.

popbooksonline.com/john-adams

*Scanning QR codes requires a web-enabled smart device with a QR code reader app and a camera.

Table of Contents

Early Life

John Adams was born in a
small town in Massachusetts
in 1735. Massachusetts
was an American **colony**
controlled by Great Britain.

Watch a video here!

John became a lawyer.

He married Abigail Smith

in 1764.

John earned a
scholarship to
Harvard College.
He was 16.

War

In 1770, a crowd of Americans attacked British soldiers in Boston. The soldiers fired shots, and people died. This was called the **Boston Massacre**.

Learn more here!

Adams supported the Americans, but he agreed to be the lawyer for the British soldiers. He thought they deserved a fair trial.

Five years later, the **American Revolutionary War** started. The colonies fought to be separate from Great Britain. Adams supported the war.

IN CONGRESS, JULY 4,
Declaration of the thirteen united States

Adams chose
Thomas Jefferson to
write the Declaration of
Independence. It said
the United States was its
own country.

Vice President

Adams helped create the
Constitution. It has rules for
the US government.
Adams became the first
vice president.

Complete an
activity here!

President

Adams became the second president. Jefferson was his vice president.

Adams was the first president to live in the White House.

Learn more here!

Adams was a **Founding Father**. He helped create the United States we know today.

Adams and Jefferson both died on July 4, 1826. This was also the 50th anniversary of the Declaration of Independence.

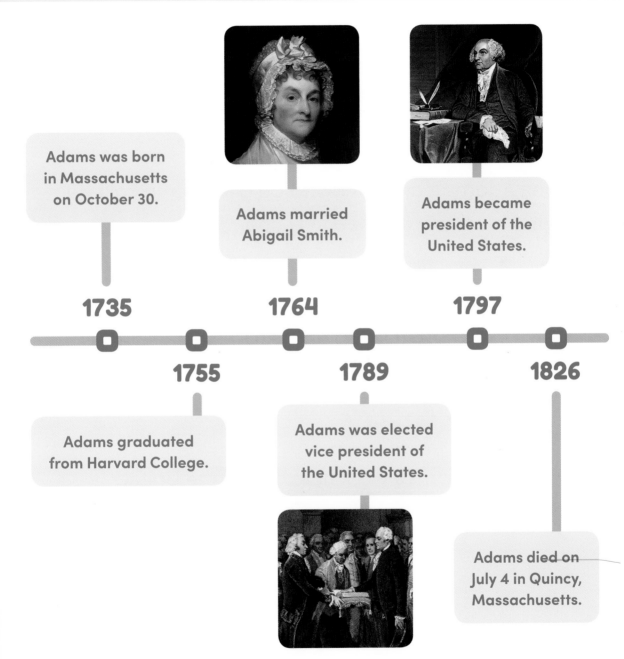

Adams was born in Massachusetts on October 30.

Adams married Abigail Smith.

Adams became president of the United States.

1735

1764

1797

1755

1789

1826

Adams graduated from Harvard College.

Adams was elected vice president of the United States.

Adams died on July 4 in Quincy, Massachusetts.

Making Connections

Text-to-Self

John Adams learned how to be a lawyer in college. What have you learned in school?

Text-to-Text

Have you read another book about someone from the past? What did you learn from it?

Text-to-World

How did Adams's work help create the United States that we live in today?

Glossary

American Revolutionary War – the war fought between the colonies and Great Britain.

Boston Massacre – an event in which British soldiers shot at colonists, causing war.

colony – land ruled by another country.

Constitution – a set of rules about what the US government can do.

Founding Father – one of the people who helped create the US government.

scholarship – money given to someone so they can attend school.

Index

Online Resources

popbooksonline.com

Thanks for reading this Cody Koala book!

Scan this code* and others like it in this book, or visit the website below to make this book pop!

popbooksonline.com/john-adams

*Scanning QR codes requires a web-enabled smart device with a QR code reader app and a camera.